DISNEP
FROZEN II

The Enchanted Forest

Adapted by
Suzanne Francis

Illustrated by the
Disney Storybook Art Team

Random House 🏠 New York

rhcbooks.com

ISBN 978-0-593-12692-9 (trade)

ISBN 978-0-593-12693-6 (lib. bdg.)

Printed in the United States of America

10 9 8 7 6 5 4 3 2 1

Chapter 1

It was early, and the light that came before the sun rose was just beginning to color the sky. The group had been walking through the night and were grateful to see that the new day was about to begin. Elsa carried an ice crystal. Powered by her magic, the crystal lit the way as Anna, Kristoff, Olaf, and Sven followed behind her.

Olaf yawned. Tired from being out all night with his friends, the snowman rode

on Sven's antlers. "Are we almost there?" he asked sleepily.

"Yes, I think so," said the brawny Kristoff. "The farm should be just a little farther past this bend." Farmer Anders, who knew Kristoff well, had immediately offered his wagon for their journey when he realized it was still not safe for them to return to Arendelle for their own.

The group followed the path as it curled around the hills in the cliffs above the village. They paused at a ridge, stopped by the sight of Arendelle, oddly quiet, below.

The unsettling view sent a shiver down Anna's spine, and she pulled her mother's scarf tightly around her shoulders. In that moment, the young princess was especially grateful to have it. The treasured scarf always seemed to give her a warm wave of comfort.

"It's so eerie," said Olaf, staring down at the deserted kingdom.

They all agreed. It was strange seeing Arendelle so lifeless. It seemed like only moments before—instead of hours—that an unseen force had driven the terrified villagers out of their homes and up to the cliffs. The villagers could not return until they figured out what was going on. Right now, it was far too dangerous.

"So . . . is the kingdom still a kingdom without anyone in it?" Olaf asked. "If there's a queen and a princess and a friendly snowman and a reindeer and a guy who talks to rocks and talks for reindeer, looking at an eerie empty kingdom . . . is that still a kingdom? I'm beginning to feel extremely uncertain about reality."

"Don't worry, Olaf," said Elsa, the queen Olaf had mentioned. "I am going to fix this, and everyone will be able to go home.

Arendelle will be just fine." Elsa kept walking, looking out into the distance. She turned to Kristoff. "Is that the farm?"

He caught up to her and nodded, letting out a small sigh. "A bit farther than I remembered, but yes. That's it."

Elsa picked up her pace as they continued

along the rocky path. Although she appeared calm, she was eager to get all that they needed and begin their journey. It wasn't only about fixing everything for Arendelle and the kingdom's people. There was also the voice. It had started as a whisper, a single note of song, that she could never quite pinpoint. She wasn't sure why, but she was certain she needed to follow the sound of the voice.

She didn't hear it at the moment, but she knew she would hear it again. For some reason that she couldn't put words to, she trusted the voice. It had helped her tap into a new part of herself and expand her power in unexpected ways. She wondered if there was even more for her to discover.

It was strange—when the voice had first

called to her, Elsa had tried to ignore it. She didn't understand. . . . *Why can no one else hear it?* she'd thought. *Is it possible that it is coming from someone magical like me?* None of the explanations she came up with made sense. So Elsa tried to convince herself that she imagined hearing it, or that the voice was just inside her head. But it had continued calling to her at unexpected moments, begging her to find it.

Earlier that night, the voice had awakened Elsa from her sleep. It had taken her a moment to clear the dreams from her head, but once she had, she sat straight up. Anna was sleeping soundly next to her, so Elsa had been careful as she sneaked out of the room. The voice continued. She followed it down

the deserted hallways of the castle and out a back door. It seemed to only grow louder and clearer as her feet touched the ground beyond the village. Unable to stay silent any longer, Elsa used her powerful voice and answered. She sang a single pure note, and something inside her shifted. She felt a connection to the voice that she had never felt before.

Tentatively, Elsa reached out with her magic. Incredible things sprang from her fingertips—she created an entire life-sized forest from snow. The deeper into the forest she wandered, the more amazed she became. With every move of her hand and every turn of her wrist, something new appeared: a swirling wind, a salamander, a water horse, and giant creatures throwing boulders.

Elsa's feet quickened as she followed the creatures that had sprung from her magic. She wanted to memorize what they looked like. She also wanted to follow them. She wanted to know where they were going.

The deeper she went into the forest of ice, the louder and more urgent the voice got. Elsa knew something was about to happen. But she had gone as far as she could—the deep waters of the fjord stood before her and kept her from reaching the voice. Elsa refocused her magic and created a wedge of ice on which she could move out over the fjord. She continued until something told her she had gone far enough.

As the voice began to fade, Elsa reached out for it, trying to bring it back. She stood

looking up at the sky, her arms at her sides, and released all her energy into the air. This caused a shock wave to blast across the fjord and turn the air's moisture into ice crystals. The crystals spread out as far as she could see, hovering in place like frozen raindrops! She couldn't hold back a smile when she realized the crystals were the result of her magical power.

Elsa noticed something special about the crystals. Each one was etched with a symbol she recognized. The symbols represented the spirits of nature: air, fire, water, and earth.

Without warning, a flash of light exploded into the sky from the north. Elsa knew the brilliance was too widespread to have been lightning, and there had been no accompanying thunder. She wondered if the light was a response to her blast of power.

As the light in the north faded, the ice crystals cascaded from the sky, falling in waves like dominoes. And as they dropped to the ground, Arendelle transformed. Water stopped flowing in the fountains, animal troughs dried up, and the kingdom went dark as the fire vanished from all the lanterns. The wind whipped angrily through windows and around corners, and the ground rippled like the sea. Those two things combined pushed everyone out of their homes, out of the kingdom, and up to the safety and stability of the cliffs.

Kristoff's voice brought Elsa's attention back to the present. They had reached the

farm. "The wagon's in the back, behind the house," Kristoff said. "Farmer Anders said we could also borrow any supplies we need from the barn. Why don't you two look in there while we go get the wagon ready." The girls nodded. "Oh, and see if you can find some carrots." Then he led Sven, with Olaf still riding on his antlers, toward the back of the farm.

Anna and Elsa entered the barn and looked around. Anna's eyes landed on a big old satchel hanging on a nearby hook. "Ooh. Perfect," she said, picking it up. She immediately placed a couple of carrots inside. As the girls collected a few more items they thought they would need, Anna kept a close eye on Elsa. As much as she trusted and believed in her sister, Anna was worried. The wise old troll, Grand Pabbie, had given Anna a secret warning after she and the others had helped evacuate Arendelle, and she couldn't stop thinking about it.

After the chaos in the village, Elsa had told Anna and Kristoff about the voice that had been calling to her. Then she asked if she could borrow a wagon so she could travel to the Enchanted Forest. Anna and Kristoff had refused to let Elsa go on the trip alone. If she was determined to go, then they were going with her. Also, they wanted to know more about the voice.

Before Elsa had time to get into more of the details, Grand Pabbie and the mountain trolls had rolled their round, rocklike bodies

through the pass, popping open as they neared the group. Pabbie had told them that he knew the spirits were awake—he could feel it. He could also feel that they were angry. Reaching up, he waved his hand around, stirring the blues and greens of the northern lights, making them brighter as he searched for answers. But it was all very mysterious, even to the wise old troll. "Much about the past is not what it seems," he had said. "A dark secret is buried too deep for me. A wrong demands resolution. Without it, I see no future." Then he had looked at Elsa urgently. "When one can see no future, all one can do is the next right thing."

Elsa had insisted that she knew the right thing to do. She had to go to the Enchanted

Forest and find the voice. She believed it was trying to help her. If she could follow it, she could fix things—she could bring the elements back to Arendelle, and she could help banish the mist from the Enchanted Forest.

Grand Pabbie and Anna had paused at Elsa's confidence. Neither had ever seen her so certain of herself before. Grand Pabbie told Elsa that she had to make sure that she was prepared. "The spirits are powerful, and they will challenge you every step of the way," he had said.

He had agreed to watch over the people of Arendelle while she and her group journeyed north to the forest. Then he had secretly pulled her sister aside. "Anna," he'd said, "I am worried for her. We have always feared that Elsa's powers were too much for this world. Now we must pray they are enough."

Anna had vowed to stay by Elsa's side no matter what.

The clop of Sven's hooves and the turn of the wagon wheels against the ground shook the girls from their thoughts. Elsa turned to face Anna. "Are you ready?" she asked.

Anna took off their mother's scarf and put it deep inside the satchel to keep it safe. "Yes," she said. She followed her sister, determined to protect her at any cost.

Chapter 2

Kristoff adjusted Sven's harness while Olaf sat excitedly in the back of the wagon, making himself comfortable in a pile of hay. "When's the last time we went on a road trip together?" he asked. "This is exciting. And I've never been to an enchanted forest before, let alone *the* Enchanted Forest. It sounds both magical *and* delightful. How long will it take us to get there?"

"Well . . . it will probably take us quite a while, Olaf," Anna said, climbing into the wagon beside him. "Our father said the Enchanted Forest is 'as north as we can go.'" She looked over at Elsa and smiled. "Remember?"

"Of course I do," said Elsa, sitting down on the other side of Olaf.

What little Anna and Elsa knew about the Enchanted Forest was from their father. Though they hadn't heard him tell the story since they were children, both girls remembered it well. It had mesmerized them and become one of their most cherished memories.

Their father, King Agnarr, had always told the story the same way: "Far away, as north as we can go, once stood an enchanted forest protected by the spirits of air, fire, water,

and earth. And there roamed a nomadic people called the Northuldra, who relied upon those spirits."

It went on about how the spirits of nature lived in harmony with the Northuldra. Once, when the kingdom of Arendelle was young, its inhabitants had put down roots on the shores of the Arenfjord. Soon after, the Arendellians met the Northuldra. The

Northuldra had seemed to welcome their new neighbors, and as a gift, the Arendellians built a great dam to connect all their lands. By bridging the wide river, the dam created a safe place for the Northuldra, and their reindeer, to cross. It was a symbol of peace.

The spirits of the Enchanted Forest remained content, and all was well. Until . . . the battle.

Thoughts of their father's story were interrupted as Kristoff climbed into the front of the wagon and grabbed Sven's reins. "All right," he said. "Everybody ready?"

Even though the sun was now barely over the horizon, its light was already reaching across the dark landscape, dispelling the shadows. Early as it was, Sven took off,

pulling the wagon northward. The leaves that had been painted with the morning light decorated everything in bright reds, oranges, and purples. It was another beautiful autumn day.

"Who's into trivia?" asked Olaf, settling in. "I am! Okay!" As the journey started, he rambled on, sharing facts and theories. Ever since he'd learned to read, he was almost never without a book. "Did you know that bees have an extra stomach? One of them is used to carry around nectar."

"Interesting," said Anna. "And sort of disgusting."

"I know!" said Olaf cheerfully. He continued chatting away: "Did you know that moonbows are just like rainbows, only

they use moonlight instead of sunlight? Did
you know that many animals use their tails
for balance but also as a blanket? But not
Sven. His tail isn't good for balance or a
blanket."

Sven grunted in disagreement.

"Oh, it's okay, buddy. Your tail is good for lots of other things!" Olaf assured him.

It wasn't long before the bright sun was high in the sky, shining down on them. Olaf sighed happily and leaned his head back on his twig arms for a moment, enjoying the

feel of the warm sun on his face.

"I love my new permafrost," he said.

He had been thoroughly enjoying Elsa's newest gift to him, which allowed him plenty of time for lounging in the sunshine. He no longer needed his personal snow flurry to keep him from melting.

"Did you know the sun is just a really, really, really, really big star?" Olaf quickly began shooting out facts again. "Did you know that storm clouds are called cumulonimbus?" He looked up into the sky. "Glad we don't see any of those now. The thin and wispy ones are called cirrus. And we don't see any of those, either. Actually, we don't see *any* clouds, do we? It *is* a really nice day, huh?"

"Uh-huh," said Anna, forcing a smile through clenched teeth. Olaf's chattering was starting to make her head ache.

"Did you know that water has memory?" said Olaf. "True fact. It's disputed but true."

Olaf continued to rattle on, and by the time they saw Elsa's ice palace, the sun was beginning to set, sparkling against the North Mountain.

"Oh! Too bad we don't have time to stop and say hello to Marshmallow and the rest of my little brothers," said Olaf, sitting up and gazing at the palace. "I wonder if they're home. Is it Wednesday? I think they're doing book club on Wednesdays now . . . or is it the knitting social? Can't remember." Olaf turned away from the scenery and reengaged with his companions in the wagon. "Okay! Back to trivia!" Everyone winced as he continued. "Did you know men are six times more likely to be struck by lightning? Sorry, Kristoff." He reached out a twig arm and patted Kristoff on the shoulder.

Kristoff forced a laugh. "I think maybe it's time for the quiet game," he suggested. His cheeks were a little red and his voice sounded mechanical.

"Out of all the games that I have tried, that one sounds like it would be my least favorite," Olaf said brightly. The ice palace disappeared over the ridge behind them

as the little snowman continued. "Did you know gorillas burp when they're happy? Did you know we blink four million times a day, and wombats poop squares, and donkeys sink but mules don't?"

Kristoff couldn't take any more. "Did you know . . . sleeping quietly on long journeys prevents murderous insanity?"

"That doesn't sound true," said Olaf with a giggle.

Elsa and Anna quickly added, "It's true. It's absolutely true."

"Huh, well, you're the grown-ups, you'd know," said Olaf. Then he yawned and cuddled between the girls, finally ready for a little nap. He soon fell asleep and Elsa waved her arms, creating a blanket of ice for him.

She made sure to tuck in all the edges.

"I'm tired, too," said Elsa. Night had fallen, and the motion of the wagon was making her sleepy.

"Take a rest," said Anna. "Here." She pulled their mother's scarf from the satchel and draped it over Elsa, comforting her instantly.

"Aww. Thank you." Elsa happily wrapped the scarf around her body, relaxing beneath it.

But Anna didn't feel tired. Once Elsa drifted off to sleep, she began to fret about something else . . . the villagers. She couldn't help thinking of them, stuck up on the cliffs, away from their homes. She knew the trolls would keep them safe, but she wondered how comfortable they would be. However, there were more immediate things to worry

about. Trying to push the villagers to the back of her mind, Anna climbed up front and sat beside Kristoff.

"They're both asleep," she said. "Hope our people are able to sleep." Suddenly, her eyes went wide. "Oh, no—do you think Mrs. Latham has her medication? And Mr. Hylton is always losing his teeth. . . ."

"Don't worry," said Kristoff. "I'm sure whatever they need, Oaken will have it and overcharge them for it."

Anna smiled appreciatively.

"You know, it's been amazing watching you care for Arendelle," Kristoff said, looking over at her with pride and love.

"I'd do anything for Arendelle," Anna said earnestly.

"Sven, keep us steady, will yah?" Sven gave a supportive grunt and Kristoff let go of the reins. He hadn't told anybody but Sven yet, but he had a secret: he was planning to ask Anna to marry him. He had tried once before, but it hadn't worked out. He had even managed to get down on one knee at the castle! And yet again Anna had been so concerned about Elsa that she didn't even see him behind her. So he had decided he would patiently wait until the timing felt completely right. And this moment felt just about as right as any.

"I want to ask you something," said Kristoff, turning toward Anna again. "It's about us. . . ."

"Oh, no," said Anna with worried frown. "What did I do?"

Kristoff was surprised by her question. "What?"

"I mean, you said it yourself: when it comes to love, I haven't had the best judgment, but—"

"I said that?" Kristoff interrupted, confused.

"When I almost married a man I just met, who did turn out to be a murderous lunatic," said Anna.

"Oh, right," Kristoff agreed. "I said that."

Kristoff didn't notice as Elsa suddenly sat up, looking around. He reached into his pocket. "Well, that's in the past. I'm talking about the future. . . ."

"Kristoff, stop, please," said Elsa.

At first he thought she wanted him to stop talking. "I can't stop the future," he said. But one look at her face made Kristoff grab the reins and guide Sven to a halt.

"I hear it," Elsa said. "I hear the voice."

Chapter 3

Elsa quickly climbed out of the back of the wagon. She walked around a bend in the path and up a hill, marveling at what she saw in the distance.

The view was so breathtaking, she wasn't even aware when the rest of the group joined her.

The morning sun softly lit the vast open field stretched out below them. In the distance, shimmering mist formed a thick barrier that was impossible to see through from where they stood. The only evidence of anything beyond the mist was the sight of trees poking out way above it, their pointed tops reaching toward the sky.

The group watched the mist as it rolled and sparkled with billowing lights—lights that Elsa felt were magical. There was no doubt in their minds—they had found the edge of the Enchanted Forest!

It was even more amazing than Anna and Elsa had imagined it would be.

As their father had told them when they were children, after the Northuldra had received the gift of the dam from the Arendellians, there'd been a great celebration and feast in the forest. He had explained, "We let down our guard. We were charmed.

It felt so . . . mystical magical. But it was a trick. The Northuldra attacked us."

He described how the wonderful celebration of peace turned into something terrible. "It was a brutal battle. The king . . . my father . . . was lost."

He went on to explain that all the fighting between the two groups had infuriated the spirits of nature. Chaos had consumed the forest. A boulder had landed at his feet, pushing him backward, and he'd hit his head on a stone and fallen unconscious. Yet he'd mysteriously managed to escape the forest. "A most haunting voice cried out. And someone saved me. . . . The spirits fell silent. And an impenetrable mist enveloped the forest, locking some in and the rest of us out."

Since that day, no one had ever entered or left the forest.

As Anna looked at the mist sparkling in the distance, her mind hung on that word: "impenetrable," meaning impossible to get through. But they *had* to get through it if Elsa was going to do the next right thing and find the voice.

Elsa suddenly gasped, breaking Anna out of her thoughts. An invisible force seemed to tug at her sister. Anna watched as Elsa quickly hurried over the ridge and down the side of the hill.

Anna, Kristoff, Olaf, and Sven hurried after her. Elsa made it to the bottom, and without looking back, the young queen darted across the field.

The others struggled to catch up. When they finally did, Elsa was standing a good distance from the edge of the mist, staring at it thoughtfully.

Kristoff slowly stepped up to the wall of gray that was keeping them out of the Enchanted Forest. He held his hand up and touched it lightly, which made it vibrate against his skin. When he pushed his hand into the mist, the mist pushed back!

Upon seeing this, Olaf's eyes lit up as a wonderful idea popped into his mind. He backed up, ran toward the mist, and jumped against it! He giggled as he bounced off its springy surface. It became a game to him as he ran at it again and again, bouncing off it as if it were a balloon!

Still gazing into the mist, Elsa took a deep breath. Then she slowly began to approach it. She paused, reached out, and grabbed Anna's hand. Holding on to her sister, she felt Anna's strength combine with her own. With that comfort, Elsa continued moving.

They walked toward the mist, and Kristoff, Sven, and Olaf joined them. The mist sparkled and rolled back a little, revealing four giant stone monoliths towering into the sky. In order to examine them more closely, they would actually have to step into the mist. But there was something about the stones that Elsa recognized, even at that distance: the symbol on each one.

"Air, fire, water, earth," she said.

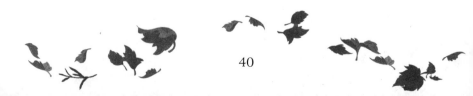

Anna turned to Elsa. "Promise me we'll do this together," she said.

"I promise," said Elsa.

They continued their journey with one step, and then another. The mist rolled back a bit more, parting and creating a passageway for them. As they moved forward, they looked around curiously. Walking through the mist was like walking into a dream.

When they made it inside the mist, the stones loomed over them. Elsa knew she had been right. The symbols carved into the pillars matched the etchings on the ice crystals she had created in Arendelle! She touched each one.

When glittering ribbons of light appeared, interwoven in the mist, the group's attention

moved from the stones. They watched the lights, mesmerized, as the colors flashed and gracefully danced before them. They were so dazzled that no one seemed to notice when the mist closed behind them, cutting off the way they had come in.

Sven grunted nervously.

"It's okay," said Kristoff, trying to calm him.

The group continued to watch, and soon the ribbons of light picked up speed, darting behind them like bolts of lightning. Then the mist began pushing against their backs— but this time, the force shoved them hard!

They all shouted as the strength of it pushed them into each other, making them run and stumble, deeper into the mist . . .

until they found themselves on the other side. They had entered the Enchanted Forest!

"What was that?" said Kristoff, shaking it off. They all turned to see that the mist sparkled with faint specks again, no longer dancing with streams of concentrated light.

Olaf grinned. He ran and jumped at it, now bouncing off the mist from the other side. Delighted, he continued to play with the trampoline-like magic.

The impenetrable mist had allowed them to enter the Enchanted Forest. But now they were trapped inside!

Chapter 4

*B*oing! *Boing! Boing!* Olaf happily bounced against the mist again and again.

"Okay, it let us in, but it clearly doesn't want to let us out," said Kristoff.

With one final bounce, Olaf fell to the ground giggling. He wiggled around, settling into the feel of the soft, cushy earth beneath him before looking up.

"Bright side—the forest is beautiful," said Elsa, admiring the view of the vibrant fall

foliage in warm reds, yellows, and oranges all around her.

Everyone agreed with Elsa; the Enchanted Forest was staggeringly exquisite. It was as if they had entered an entirely different world. They slowly walked around, taking in its natural beauty. It was absolutely stunning.

Elsa inhaled a deep breath. The air was fresh, and the forest was quiet, calm, and still. She looked up, in awe of the giant trees stretching so high, the tops disappearing in the mist. *These must be the trees I saw when I was outside on the plain!* she thought. That was when she noticed she couldn't see even one bit of sky. The mist blocked it completely.

The bit of light from the sun that filtered through the mist made the colors of the forest shimmer with a warm glow. Star moss in all shades of green covered the ground like a soft carpet, and tiny patches of vibrant flowers and ferns peeked out from behind rocks and trees.

Sven scratched his back against a wide, sturdy tree trunk, feeling its thick bark dig into his fur. Then he spotted another one to try and went over to test it out. He continued to go from tree to tree, scratching his back against each one as he passed.

The golden leaves of one tree captivated Kristoff. The young man examined them closely, intrigued. They seemed unreal, dangling delicately from beautiful arching white branches.

Anna followed the shifting rays of

sunlight cutting through the mist, sparkling with color and life as they led her over a small hill. She looked down and gasped at the remarkable sight. "The dam," she said. "It still stands."

Kristoff went to her and looked out, appreciating the view.

Anna couldn't help thinking about her father's story and the battle between the Northuldra and the Arendellians. She wondered why the Northuldra would attack her people after the Arendellians had built the dam for them so that the two lands would be joined, and there would be more room for their reindeer to roam without crossing the treacherous river. It was one part of the story that had bothered her ever since she was a child. *Where did the peace between the two groups go wrong?* she thought. That part of the story seemed to be missing.

"Still in good shape," said Kristoff, gazing out at the dam. "Thank goodness."

"What do you mean?" asked Anna, confused.

"Well, if that dam broke, it would send a tidal wave so big, it would wash away everything on this fjord," he explained.

"Arendelle's on this fjord," said Anna, her voice rising with worry.

"Nothing's gonna happen to Arendelle, Anna," said Kristoff, putting his arm around her. "It's going to be fine. Come here."

Comforted, Anna leaned into him. She wrapped her arms around him, cuddling

close. The two looked out, silently enjoying the view together for a moment, listening to the sound of the rushing water in the distance.

An idea came to Kristoff. He reached into his pocket and dug around for the ring he had for Anna. It was made of gold with a special stone set in it that he had gotten from his troll family. Kristoff knew Anna would love it, and he was excited to give it to her, but he wanted the moment to be perfect—one they would both remember forever.

Clasping the ring tightly in his palm, he thought it was time to try—again.

"You know," he said, "under different circumstances, this would be a pretty romantic place. Don't you think?"

"Different circumstances?" asked Anna, turning to look up at him, worry in her expression. "You mean, like . . . with someone else?"

"What?" Kristoff asked, wondering how Anna would even ask that. Somehow, things had taken a turn for the worse. He knew he had to hurry. "No, no. I'm saying . . . just in case we don't make it out of here . . ."

Anna pulled away and stared at him with a frown. "Wait, what? You don't think we're going to make it out of here?"

"No. No!" said Kristoff, trying to laugh off her concern. "I mean, we *will* make it out of here." He rambled nervously, "Well, technically, the odds are kinda complicated. But my point is, in case we die—"

"You think we are going to die?" asked Anna, interrupting him again.

"No!" Kristoff said, realizing once again that the proposal was not going as he had intended. For some reason, he just couldn't seem to find the right words to get back on track. He knew another chance was slipping away, making him fumble even more. "No, no, no, we will die at some point, but not at any recent time will we die, but way far in the future, we will die—"

Anna suddenly realized she didn't see her sister anywhere. "Where's Elsa?" she blurted, panicked. "I swore I wouldn't leave her side!" She abruptly ran off into the woods, shouting Elsa's name.

Kristoff sighed. Sven, who had been

watching nearby, stepped up beside him. Kristoff looked over at the reindeer. "I'm fine," he said quickly.

But Sven had been Kristoff's friend for too long, and he knew that Kristoff was anything but fine. He rubbed his muzzle against his friend's shoulder, trying to comfort him.

Anna frantically ran back toward the edge of the Enchanted Forest and began to search for her sister. But Elsa was nowhere to be found!

Chapter 5

"Elsa!" Anna's voice rang out through the forest. She picked up speed as she looked behind bushes and over ridges, her voice growing louder with concern.

Elsa didn't hear her sister calling. She was walking among the giant trees, lost in thought. She closed her eyes and took a deep breath of the crisp air.

But she sensed something. There was a prickling sensation on the back of her neck, and her eyes shot open. She spun around

immediately, ready to face whatever was following her.

At that moment, Anna rushed to her side. Elsa was surprised when she saw Anna.

"Elsa! There you are!" she said, thrilled to

see that her sister was safe. "You okay?"

"I'm fine," Elsa answered distantly.

Anna breathed a sigh of relief. "Okay. Good." But the moment of calm didn't last long. Anna looked around, again wearing a worried expression. "Where's Olaf?"

The two of them glanced in every direction but didn't see the little snowman anywhere. The girls joined forces with Kristoff and Sven and immediately began searching the area.

Off in a distant part of the woods, Olaf happily skipped across the forest floor. He was thoroughly enjoying exploring every inch of the amazing, magical, delightful place. "Anyone else feel like they're being watched?" he asked, not realizing he had strayed so far from his group. "Anyone? No one? I'm alone."

Olaf looked around, wondering where everyone had gone.

"Anna? Elsa? Sven? Samantha?" He cracked up, chuckling to himself. "I don't even know a Samantha," he added.

Just then, a strong gust of wind whooshed by. It rushed behind him, sending a shiver up his back.

"Whoa," Olaf said, spinning around, thinking someone was there. Seeing nobody, he shrugged it off.

CRACK! A thick branch above him split and made a loud popping noise. Then a pile of leaves fell on his head!

"That's normal," said Olaf, shaking them

off. He didn't want to admit it, but he was starting to feel a little bit nervous.

As he started to walk away, a rock fell right in front of him. It had seemed to come from nowhere, causing him to trip. He fell flat on his face and got a mouthful of dirt. Before he could get up, a geyser burst from the ground beneath him! The water soaked him as it pushed him back up to standing.

Olaf remained still for a moment, wondering exactly what was going on. Then he heard something scampering in the trees above. "What was that?" he asked, cautiously looking up.

As he continued walking, the earth before him broke open, and suddenly he was staring down into what looked like an endless black

hole! He slowly backed away from the edge of the pit. "Samantha?" he asked, his voice now quaking with fear.

The realization that he was alone in a strange place finally hit him. The Enchanted

Forest didn't seem so amazing, magical, and delightful now—it was terrifying!

A black line that sizzled with heat sent up smoke as it burned straight through a lush mound of star moss. It picked up speed, charring everything in its path, zooming toward him! He leaped out of the way a moment before the black line could run across his leg.

Struggling to calm his nerves, he told

60

himself that everything he was experiencing was normal. Olaf was sure that if his grown-up friends were there, they would tell him things were completely fine. He was certain that when he grew up, he would know all kinds of things he didn't yet know, like that everything happening in the forest right now was *not* out of the ordinary. Olaf would later look back on this and laugh. It would all make sense to him in the future—he was sure of it!

Keeping a positive outlook, he walked through a thick cluster of trees, trying to find his way back to the group. Vines twisted around gnarled tree branches above and around him, making the area dark and spooky. But Olaf bravely pressed on.

Several pairs of glowing eyes peered out at him, staring through bushes. He could only imagine the creatures behind those creepy gazes. Olaf winced and said weakly, "Excuse me," trying hard to remain polite even as he fought to keep it together. He hurried ahead.

Olaf came upon a clearing with a small stream. He looked at his reflection in the water, hoping the sight would be a comfort. But his face looked warped and weird in the creek's ripples. It only made him feel worse.

Then Olaf's reflection changed. Now he was looking at a strange creature. Olaf touched his face, but it felt the same. He suddenly realized that the creature wasn't him—it was something that was staring up at him from beneath the surface of water! Unable to stay

calm for another second, he let out a loud shriek. "AAAAAAAAAHHHHHHHH!"

Sparks immediately erupted, causing a nearby bush to burst into crackling flames. Olaf took one look and screamed even louder!

The snowman's screams ended only when he ran out of breath. Oddly, the fire instantly went out, too. Olaf looked at the smoldering bushes, smoking and charred from the burn, and tilted his head curiously. He forced a small smile, reassuring himself once again that one day he would understand that all these things had a perfectly logical explanation, just like the facts he liked to quote. But one thing he truly understood at that moment was that he needed to find Elsa and the others.

Olaf looked up and saw trees swaying nearby. Then more trees began to move, and he could sense the strong wind whooshing and whirling, shoving the trees aside as it picked up speed . . . making its way toward him.

"This is fine," he said, even as his eyes got bigger.

And when the wind reached him, it swooped Olaf up and tossed him into the air! It swirled him all around, separating his body parts and sending them flying every which way. Olaf did the only thing he could—he cried out for his friends!

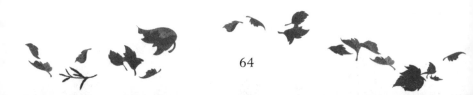

Chapter 6

When they heard Olaf's calls for help, the group rushed to find him. They were shocked to see his parts swooshing and whooshing around in the air. Olaf was thrilled to see everyone! But just then, the wind grabbed at his friends and swept them up, too! They flailed and flopped as they were flung through the air like giant juggling balls! The wind whipped everything else in its path, too. Leaves, twigs, and dust swirled inside the giant cyclone.

Olaf's head flew by and cheerfully said, "Hey, guys!"

"Coming through," said Kristoff, sailing past Elsa.

But Elsa barely noticed. Instead, she was reminded of how the wind in Arendelle had pushed the villagers out of their homes. She realized that the wind that held them now was probably one of the spirits of the Enchanted Forest.

When Anna's skirt blew over her head, she was grateful that she was also wearing pants. The Wind Spirit spun her wildly, like a top. "I think I'm going to be sick!" she said, groaning.

Olaf's smiling face swung by again. "I'd hold your hair back, but I can't find my arms!" he exclaimed.

Kristoff and Sven zipped around inside the twister in different directions. They collided and were forced even higher inside the chaos. Kristoff grumbled as he tried to grab hold of Sven. Sven stretched toward him, but the Wind Spirit made it difficult for them to control their movements. It looked like they were performing an unusual dance.

A thick tree branch snapped off with a loud *CRACK!* and was sucked into the whirlwind. Elsa gasped when she saw it zip toward Anna. Without a second thought, Elsa used her power to flip the branch out of the cyclone before it slammed into her sister!

While it seemed that no one else noticed

what Elsa had done, the Wind Spirit did. Its velocity and force changed, and it began swirling around her hands as if it were curious.

"Hey, stop!" shouted Elsa.

Then, with an enormous *whoosh,* the Wind Spirit blew Kristoff, Sven, Anna, and all of Olaf's parts from its grasp! They tumbled to the ground.

As they rose to their feet and tried to get their bearings, they saw that Elsa was still wrapped inside the cyclone. It twisted and whipped around faster and faster, tightening its grip on her.

"Elsa!" Anna shouted, still feeling dizzy from all the spinning. She, Kristoff, and Sven tried to get close to Elsa, but the Wind Spirit was too powerful, and it pushed them back. They tried again and again, but the Wind Spirit knocked them away every time. They couldn't get anywhere near the twister.

Elsa knew she had to do something. She raised her arms and summoned her ice power, cautiously releasing a steady stream of snow. As the snow mixed with the wind, it turned to slush and the cyclone began to slow. Soon she was spinning in a thick white blur. The twister continued to solidify and slow down—but Elsa was still trapped inside.

She felt strange in the slushy funnel. It suddenly seemed that she was in another world. Mysterious sounds rang out all around her, mixing with the vibration of the wet snow rushing by. She could hear human

voices, animal noises, and what sounded like echoes of the Enchanted Forest. Some of the sounds were clear and appeared to be snippets of conversations. She found herself lost in it all, listening and eager to hear more.

Her eyes shot open when she distinctly heard a man's voice urgently cry, "Prince Agnarr!"

The sound of her father's name snapped her back to the present moment and reminded her of her important mission. She had to focus, find the mysterious voice, and return the elements of air, fire, water, and earth to Arendelle. But the first thing she had to do was find her way out of the bizarre storm.

Closing her eyes, she drew a deep breath and gathered all her power. She threw her

arms open wide and flooded the windstorm with her magic!

She heard another voice say "For Arendelle" just as the wind stopped and a blindingly bright FLASH of white appeared. Snow filled the air, and for a moment, everything was utterly still.

The group stood staring at the endless sea of white. The heavy fall of snow blocked out everything, making it impossible to see what lay before them.

Chapter 7

As the snowfall thinned to gentle flurries, the group looked around. Beautiful statues made of ice were scattered everywhere. It was as if the friends had suddenly been transported to a wintery sculpture garden, with Elsa, the sculptures' creator, standing at the very center.

The life-size statues looked like they had been carved by a master sculptor. They were incredibly detailed and conveyed life and emotion. There was a young Arendellian soldier wearing a courageous expression, holding his sword and shield high, battling an unseen opponent. There were two Northuldra women fiercely racing forward, holding their staffs firmly above them. There were two soldiers huddled together. Every sculpture told its own story.

"What are these?" asked Kristoff.

"They look like moments in time," said Elsa, fascinated. Just like the other night in Arendelle, being inside the windstorm had helped her power grow in a new, mysterious way. She couldn't believe her magic had created such amazing works of art.

Anna turned to Olaf. "What's that thing you say, Olaf?" she asked.

He smiled. "Oh! My theory about

advancing technology as both our savior and our doom?"

Anna shook her head. "No, not the . . . not that one. The one about—"

"The one about cucumbers?" Olaf asked excitedly, eager to discuss his thoughts on the delightful crunchy green thing and whether it was a fruit or a vegetable.

"No, the thing about water," said Anna.

"Oh, yeah," said Olaf. "Water has memory. True fact. It's disputed but true."

They looked at the statues again, wondering if they were looking at actual moments in time. Each sculpture was so realistic, it seemed possible. The friends wondered whether each represented something that had really happened—and

whether the people had once been real.

Anna scanned the surrounding statues, wondering if they could provide answers to the many questions she still had about the Enchanted Forest and her father's story.

Just then, the Wind Spirit returned, sweeping gently around Olaf.

"Oh, the wind's back," he said. "I think I'll name you Gale."

Everybody tensed, preparing for another possible storm as Gale breezed around Anna and lifted Elsa off her feet. Elsa quickly realized the wind was no longer aggressive.

"Ooh, oh. I'm okay. I'm okay," she said as Gale put her down.

The Wind Spirit swirled around the ice sculptures. "Did you want me to make these?" Elsa asked. Gale rattled some leaves together as if in response to the question.

Then Gale created a small opening in the trees, begging the group to move toward a sculpture that stood apart from the rest. The friends curiously formed a half circle around it.

The statue portrayed a very dramatic scene of a boy being carried in the arms of a girl. The boy appeared to be unconscious as the girl cradled him. The girl's expression was one of concern and determination.

Suddenly, Anna gasped. "Father?" she said,

looking at the statue's face. The features were very distinct—she was certain it was King Agnarr as a boy. "That's Father," she repeated, gently touching its icy surface.

Elsa leaned in and nodded. Then she looked closely at the young girl. She could see the girl was struggling with the weight of the prince. She could also see the fortitude reflected in the girl's face that would see her through the crisis.

"This girl," Elsa said. "How—"

"She's saving him," interrupted Olaf.

"She's Northuldra," said Kristoff.

Elsa and Anna exchanged a look. The story of their father mysteriously making it out of the Enchanted Forest on the day of the battle popped into their minds. They had always wondered who had saved their father. Even he hadn't known. "Somehow, someone saved me . . . ," he'd said while telling the story. It looked like this statue was showing

them who that someone was—a Northuldra girl!

The sisters were shocked to think that a Northuldra—one of the people who had supposedly tricked the Arendellians—had rescued their father on the day of the battle. One of his enemies had helped him escape the forest so he could get home to Arendelle and become king. They had a *Northuldra* to thank for saving their father?

Just then, a loud whooshing noise shook them from their thoughts.

"What is that?" Anna asked, looking around suspiciously. The sound seemed to be coming from the trees.

As they backed away from the sculpture of Prince Agnarr and the girl, the whooshing sound filled the air. Olaf let out a squeal and hid behind Anna, pulling her mother's scarf from the satchel and wrapping it around himself like a blanket as he attempted to hide.

The noise continued and was soon joined by a loud banging. The noise got increasingly faster and louder until it seemed to surround them.

The tall bushes in front of them trembled and shook. Something was hiding in them!

Anna whipped around and cracked an ice sword off one of the sculptures. She held it high and in one swift move swung it down, slicing through the thick shrubbery and revealing a group of . . . Northuldra!

They were standing beside a herd of

reindeer and held their staffs protectively. More Northuldra dropped from the trees.

A young Northuldra woman named Honeymaren stepped up to Anna and said firmly, "Lower your weapon." She held her staff up, waiting for Anna to comply.

But before Anna could react, the clanging of swords slamming against shields pierced the silence! Five Arendellian soldiers appeared behind the group, poised and ready to fight.

A lieutenant stood strong as he faced the Northuldra. His uniform was old and faded, like the uniforms of the other soldiers, but it was clear that he was still very much in charge. "And you lower yours," he commanded in a deep voice.

Chapter 8

"Arendellian soldiers?" Anna muttered to herself, finding it very odd to see them in the Enchanted Forest. She wondered . . . could these Arendellians and Northuldra be the people from their father's story who had been trapped in the Enchanted Forest when the mist rose?

A stern-looking Northuldra woman named Yelana appeared next to the lieutenant. She held her staff firmly at his side. He winced and rolled his eyes. It was

obvious that he didn't need to turn around to know who was there.

"Threatening my people again, Lieutenant?" Yelana asked.

"Invading my dance space again, Yelana?" he said sarcastically.

Anna squinted at the lieutenant. "Why does that soldier look so familiar?" she said to herself. She was certain she had seen him somewhere before . . . but where? She stepped toward him for a closer look.

Seeing that she was still holding the ice sword, one of the other Arendellian soldiers shouted, "Look out, Lieutenant!"

The soldiers instantly darted toward Anna and her group. The Northuldra took the opportunity to push in, too. Now the friends were completely surrounded.

"Get the sword!" commanded the lieutenant. He and Yelana scooted back and forth with their arms out, trying to block each other from getting to Anna's sword. But before any of them could get any closer, Elsa used her power to cover the ground beneath their feet with a layer of ice! The display of magic shocked them all.

The approaching Northuldra and Arendellians tried to move toward Anna, Elsa, and their friends, but they crashed into each other and fell, slipping and sliding all over the place.

The lieutenant gasped, staring at Elsa.

"That was magic," he said to Yelana, who had landed on the ground as well. "Did you see that?"

"Of course I saw it," said Yelana.

A young Northuldra man named Ryder
smiled over at his sister, Honeymaren.
"Explains the ice sculptures," he said with
a grin.

Ryder carefully crawled across the ice on his hands and knees. He looked up as he came face to face with Olaf. The little snowman smiled.

"And the talking snowman?" said Ryder.

"Hi. I'm Olaf," he said.

"Hi, uh, I'm Ryder. This is my sister, Honeymaren," Ryder responded. Honeymaren, who sat on the ground behind her brother, smiled slightly and gave an awkward wave.

Anna's eyes were still fixed on the lieutenant. She stared at him as she searched her memory, trying to place his face. When he rose to his feet, she finally asked, "Do I know you?"

"Have you been in this forest before?" he said. It was clear that she did not look familiar to him.

"No. Hang on a minute," she said, dropping the ice sword to the ground. She held up her hands, using her fingers to frame his face. She closed one eye and then the other, checking him out from different angles.

"This is different," he said as he waited patiently for her to finish.

Finally, she gasped. "That's it!" she cried.

"Lieutenant Mattias! Library, second portrait on the left. You were our father's official guard."

Mattias looked at Anna, shocked. "Your father was—"

"King Agnarr of Arendelle," said Elsa.

Gripping their staffs, the Northuldra took a step back, falling into a defensive line. They eyed the group suspiciously, wondering if what they were hearing was correct.

Lieutenant Mattias couldn't believe that Anna and Elsa were King Agnarr's daughters. But as surprised as he was, he was thrilled to hear that the prince had gotten out of the forest on that terrible day.

"Agnarr," he said, his voice quaking with

emotion. "He made it home to Arendelle."

"He did," said Anna. "He was a great king."

"I knew he would be . . . ," said Mattias. "Wait." He looked at the girls with concern. "'Was'?"

"Our father and mother were lost on a voyage in the Southern Sea seven years ago," explained Elsa.

The Arendellian soldiers silently bowed their heads, paying a moment of respect to their lost king and queen.

Mattias took a deep breath and then smiled sweetly.

"I see him," he said gently. "I see him in your faces."

"Really?" said Anna, genuinely touched. It suddenly hit her that she had forgotten her manners. "I'm Anna, and this is my sister, Queen Elsa."

Mattias nodded to them.

Yelana stepped up, irritated. "Why are you here?" she asked.

"A powerful magic forced our people out of our kingdom—" explained Anna.

"To protect them," Elsa interrupted.

"From what?" Mattias asked.

Anna looked at Elsa and then back at Mattias. "All we know is it has something to do with whatever happened in this forest."

"None of us knows what really happened in this forest," said a soldier.

"What spells did you use to awaken the spirits, to get through the mist?" Yelana asked accusingly.

"No spells," said Elsa. "Someone called to me. Someone let us in. They have answers, I know it—answers that can get us out of here."

Everyone began whispering excitedly.

"Don't trust her or her sorcery," said Yelana, turning toward her people.

"She doesn't use sorcery," said Anna. "She was born with magic!"

A silence fell over the crowd.

"Impossible," said Yelana, spitting out the word with anger. "Why would nature reward a person of Arendelle with such power?"

Mattias glared at Yelana, moving toward her. "To make up for the actions of *your* people."

"*My* people?" Yelana asked, outraged. "My people came in good faith to honor the dam. Your people used the dam to trick us!"

"The dam was a gift of peace," said Mattias.

"Or was it a gift of hate?" Yelana asked.

"You'd like to see it fall. You'd like to see Arendelle washed away," Mattias said.

Yelana shook her head. "I don't have such hate in me." She turned to Elsa. "But did you know that your grandfather, your king, despised magic?"

Anna and Elsa were both shocked to hear Yelana say such a thing about their grandfather.

"He only feared how people like you could exploit it," said Mattias. "And you killed him for it!"

"You can't prove that!" shouted Yelana.

"The spirits themselves turned against you!" shouted Mattias.

The tension between the two leaders was rising once again.

"They turned on you, too!" yelled Yelana, shaking a finger at him angrily. "YOU ARE TRAPPED HERE, TOO!"

A blinding flash of light cut through the arguing, making everyone fall silent. Then a bright fireball whipped out from behind a tree and vanished in a blur. Everyone spun around, bracing for whatever was going to happen next.

There was a deafening *BOOM,* and an enormous tree burst into flames! It crackled as the blaze grew, lapping up everything around it, quickly enveloping the tree and all the nearby brush.

"FIRE SPIRIT!" cried Yelana.

Chapter 9

Olaf backed away, fearfully eyeing the crackling flames. "This will all make sense when I am older," he whispered to himself, trying to remain calm.

"Get back, everyone!" ordered Yelana.

"Head for the river!" shouted Mattias.

The fireball zipped and zoomed around at an incredible pace, leaving disaster in its wake. As it zigzagged across the Northuldra camp, people screamed and dove out of the way. Elsa ran to help. Magic poured out of

her hands in waves as she tried to put out the flames. The ferocious fire was too much. It continued to grow and spread, picking up speed as it ripped through the camp. Elsa's power didn't seem to have any effect on it. Her ice magic didn't even slow it down!

Ryder noticed the herd of reindeer running from the fire, but in the wrong direction! Panicked, he shouted, "No, no, no. The reindeer! That's a dead end!"

"Come on, Sven," Kristoff said bravely. Then he called to Ryder, "We'll get them!" He climbed onto Sven's back and they bolted toward the reindeer, ready to lead them in a safer direction.

A wall of flames suddenly blocked their path—there was no way to get to the reindeer!

Seeing them trapped, Elsa used her power to blast a temporary icy opening in the fire just big enough for Sven and Kristoff to squeeze through. They leaped between the flames as soon as they could and took off after the frightened herd.

Anna, who had been helping the Northuldra evacuate their camp, looked back to see Elsa trying to battle huge flames that towered over her. "Elsa! Get out of there!" she yelled.

Anna turned and pushed her way through the people heading in the opposite direction. She was determined to enter the chaos and get to Elsa.

The fire roared as it spread, burning faster than Anna could run. Before she knew it, it had closed in on her. She coughed, trying to call to her sister even as her voice began to fail.

Kristoff had reached the herd and Sven reared up, both of them fearful as they put themselves between the reindeer and the growing flames. "Come on, buddy," said Kristoff, encouraging him. "We can do this." He steadied himself and held on tight. "Hiya!" he shouted, taking off. One quick glance over his shoulder made him smile. The herd had fallen in behind Sven and were following him to safety.

Caught in the flames, Anna suddenly fell to her knees. She struggled to breathe as the fire continued to close in. Kristoff saw her and shouted, "Anna!" to Elsa, to draw her attention to her sister.

Hearing Kristoff's cry, Elsa spun around. She blasted her magic into the blaze, creating another opening for Kristoff. He and Sven dashed through, and in one fell swoop, Kristoff grabbed Anna and hoisted her up onto Sven's back. They galloped away from the fire.

"Get her out of here!" yelled Elsa.

"No, Elsa!" shouted Anna, looking toward her sister with concern. She wanted to jump down and join her, to protect her. She had vowed to stay by her side, and here she was, being carried off in the opposite direction! Despite Anna's pleas, Kristoff continued. Anna watched desperately as Elsa turned and disappeared between massive waves of hot flame.

Elsa kept working hard with her magic, courageously battling the fire. But no matter what she did, the fire did not get any smaller. She changed strategies and chased after the moving fireball until suddenly, it seemed to diminish at a small rocky cliff. It appeared to roll beneath the rocks.

Seeing that the Fire Spirit was finally contained, she slowed and caught her breath. Then she spotted something. She leaned in close and saw a pair of terrified eyes peering out at her. The Fire Spirit was a small salamander!

Elsa watched as the salamander whimpered and coughed, sending out a steady stream of fire that shot toward a tree.

Waving her hands, Elsa gave the blaze

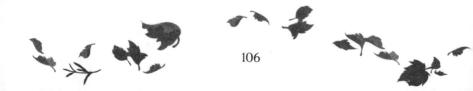

a blast of magic. She and the salamander watched as the orange flames sparked and fizzled with color before freezing in midair. The icy fire looked strange and beautiful as it hung there for a single moment before melting away.

The salamander looked up at Elsa. The Fire Spirit's expression was cautious and wary, as if it were afraid of being hurt.

Elsa gently held out her hand, and the salamander walked toward it. The creature slowly approached her, carefully stretching one leg in front of the other, keeping its eyes on her the whole time. The salamander crept onto her hand, one foot at a time, easing along her cool skin. Small smoldering flames continued to rise from its back.

Elsa winced as she felt the salamander's flaming-hot skin. But she took a deep breath, letting the little animal cool off in her hand. "Oh!" she whispered as the salamander sizzled in her palm. "Ow, ow."

She raised her other hand and sprinkled some snowflakes in front of the creature. As the little salamander gobbled them up, the flames on its back went out. The more it relaxed, the more the small fires still crackling in the brush around them died down.

Elsa continued to create more snowflakes in the air for the salamander. Now completely cooled off, the salamander playfully shot out a tiny burst of fire, popping the snowflakes into little puffs of steam. Elsa made more

and the salamander did it again, enjoying the fun little game.

All of the fires around them smoked gently now, finally out. The salamander happily snuggled deeper into Elsa's hand. Elsa smiled, feeling especially connected to the little creature.

The sudden sound of footsteps nearby brought Elsa back to her surroundings. She turned and peeked over her shoulder to see several Northuldra and the Arendellian soldiers standing there, staring curiously and whispering to each other.

"They're all looking at us, aren't they?" she said softly to the salamander. "Got any advice? No? Nothing?" The salamander flicked out its tongue, licking its eyes. "Hmm, should I know what that means?"

Just then, she heard the voice!

It hadn't called to her since before she'd seen the mist at the edge of the forest, but now it was loud and insistent.

She and the salamander simultaneously whipped their heads around, turning toward it!

Chapter 10

Noticing the salamander's reaction, Elsa asked, "You hear it, too?" She had thought she was the only one who heard the voice! She wondered what else she and the little creature might have in common. "Somebody's calling us. Who is it? What do we do?"

The salamander hopped out of her hand and scurried to the top of a large boulder. It looked out into the distance for a moment. Then it locked eyes with her.

"Okay, keep going north," she said, understanding the Fire Spirit.

The salamander's skin glowed brightly for a moment. It paused before turning away. Elsa watched as her new little friend leaped off the boulder, briefly suspended in the air before landing on the ground below. The salamander scampered off, disappearing into the brush.

Anna, who had been looking for Elsa, was overjoyed to see her. She ran to her and drew her into her arms, hugging her tightly. Elsa hugged her back, relieved to see that her sister was okay.

"Elsa! Oh, thank goodness!" cried Anna.

"Anna," said Elsa, holding her close. Then

she pulled away and looked at Anna with a frown. "What were you doing? You could have been killed! You can't just follow me into fire."

"You don't want me to follow you into fire, then don't run into fire! You're not being careful, Elsa!" Anna said angrily.

Kristoff walked up with Sven behind him, Olaf perched on Sven's back. Kristoff watched the girls from a distance, concerned.

Elsa could see the worry on Anna's face. "I'm sorry. Are you okay?" she asked.

"I've been better," said Anna.

"Wait, I know what you need." Elsa pulled their mother's scarf out of the satchel and wrapped it around Anna's shoulders.

The Northuldra standing nearby gasped at the sight of it and began whispering to each other. Anna and Elsa looked at them curiously.

"Where did you get that scarf?" asked Yelana.

"That's a Northuldra scarf," Ryder said, stepping toward them.

"What?" said Anna, confused.

The information sent a wave of shock through the camp as the Northuldra continued to whisper, staring at the girls and the scarf.

"Scarves like these were given to a child at birth," explained Honeymaren. "This is from one of our oldest families."

Elsa instantly thought of the sculpture of their young father in the arms of the Northuldra girl . . . the one the Wind Spirit had shown them. She grabbed Anna's hand and everyone followed as she led the way to it.

Anna and Elsa stood beside the ice sculpture, looking at it closely. Anna touched the scarf made of ice, surprised that she hadn't noticed it before. She gently caressed the girl's face with gratitude and respect.

They realized they really *must* be looking at a moment from the past. The scarf was the proof! The Northuldra girl portrayed in the sculpture must have been the reason their father had survived. The scarf had surely been hers. It was staggering to think that the scarf had originally belonged to the girl whose likeness they were staring at . . . the girl who had saved their father.

Anna and Elsa understood that the girl must have given the scarf to their father. Their mother had cherished the scarf not for its beauty, but as a reminder of the girl who had saved her husband and allowed the young king to return home.

The Northuldra and the Arendellians stood by, gawking at Anna and Elsa as well as the sculpture. They were stunned that the two opposing sides had such a powerful positive connection. They could hardly believe that on that terrible day of battle, a young Northuldra and a young Arendellian had shared peace and compassion.

Suddenly, the Wind Spirit blew through the trees, creating a beautiful clinking sound. The ice sculptures twinkled and glistened with a magical glow. Owls and other night creatures began to call out, creating a strange, harmonious symphony.

Quietly at first, and then increasingly louder, the Northuldra began singing along with the night. The Arendellian soldiers

stood around the edges, on guard, as one at a time, each Northuldra placed a hand on the shoulder of the person in front of them, forming a large triangle.

Anna and Elsa watched, mesmerized by the soothing music and the motion of the people swaying with the trees. As the Northuldra linked together and joined voices, the forest seemed to respond with an energy that the people could feel on their skin and in their bones. The sound grew in intensity, filling the air with music.

Eager to join in, Olaf put one twig hand on Kristoff and one on Sven as he tried to sing along.

Yelana, overwhelmed by the beautiful sounds, stood at the front of her people and

tenderly took Anna's and Elsa's hands in her own. Looking deep into their eyes, she said quietly, "When nature speaks, we listen. We are called Northuldra. We are the people of the sun."

The girls nodded. "We will do whatever it takes to free this forest," said Elsa.

Anna glanced over at Mattias, who wore an expression of doubt. "And to restore Arendelle," she said sincerely.

Hopeful sounds rumbled from the people. "We're getting out of here!" Ryder shouted joyfully. "What?" he said when others around him began to laugh. He turned to Kristoff, who stood next to him. "Some of us were born here. We've never even seen an open sky."

Ryder's excitement was contagious, and it spread among both the Northuldra and the Arendellian soldiers.

"I heard the voice again," Elsa told Yelana with a smile. "We need to go north."

"The Earth Giants roam the north at night," said Mattias.

"They sleep by day," explained Yelana. "You can leave in the morning."

Elsa didn't want to wait—she was too excited. But couldn't put her family or anyone in the forest at risk, so she agreed. She slowly nodded, wondering how she could wait through the night.

Chapter 11

Later, they all gathered at the Northuldra camp for dinner. A lovely fire burned and the atmosphere was cheerful. Everyone enjoyed some peaceful time together, eating and chatting. The mood was high, as they all believed that Elsa's presence, and the fact that she had been born with magic, meant they would soon be out of the Enchanted Forest. She had to be the one who could free them after all the years they had been

trapped. Even Yelana and Mattias managed to avoid bickering with each other.

Olaf played with a group of Northuldra toddlers. They surrounded him, having a blast pulling, chewing on, and rearranging his parts.

"Hey, let me ask you," said Olaf happily. "How do you guys cope with the ever-increasing complexity of thought that comes with matur—"

One of the kids grabbed Olaf's carrot nose off his face and stuck it straight up his own nose. They all cracked up.

"Brilliant!" Olaf exclaimed above the laughter. "It is so refreshing to get to talk to folks my own age," he added.

Some of the children sucked on Olaf's

feet, enjoying the feeling of the cold snow on their gums.

"No, no, no, don't chew that," said Olaf, trying to pull away. "You don't know what I've stepped in."

Anna stood with Mattias, having a bowl of stew under the starless night. Being in a magical forest where the mist blocked out the sky still seemed odd to her, but she noticed how bits of moonlight managed to break through. Shining down, it gave pieces of the forest a beautiful blue and silvery glow.

Anna enjoyed talking to Mattias about her father and Arendelle. While they chatted, Mattias kept a watchful eye on their surroundings, constantly on guard. He had

been a soldier for so many years that it came naturally to him. Plus, he had lived in the Enchanted Forest long enough to know that unexpected things often happened. Although meeting new people—one who was magical and one who was a talking snowman—was the most unexpected thing that had ever happened, either in the Enchanted Forest or outside it.

"He was about your height," said Anna.

"That tall, huh," said Mattias, trying to imagine the young prince as an adult.

"You meant a lot to him." A smile crossed her face as she continued. "Whenever we'd get butter biscuits from Blodgets' Bakery, he'd say, 'Lieutenant Mattias could never get enough of these.'" She laughed at the memory.

"It's the butter . . . ," said Mattias, closing his eyes briefly, recalling the taste of the delicious biscuits melting in his mouth. Then he glanced over at Anna. "Hey, tell me—is Halima still over at Hudson's Hearth?"

"She is," answered Anna.

"Really? She married?" he asked.

Anna shook her head no.

"Oh, wow," he said, wearing a slightly sad expression. "Why doesn't that make me feel better?"

"What else do you miss?" asked Anna. Even though they had been gone only a few days, she was missing Arendelle, too. It comforted her to talk about it.

"My father," Mattias said, looking out into the distance. "He passed long before all this.

He was a great man. Built us a good life in Arendelle, but taught me to never take the good for granted." He cleared his throat and imitated his father's voice as he continued, "He'd say, 'Be prepared. Just when you think you've found your way, life will throw you onto a new path.'"

"What do you do when it does?" asked Anna.

"Don't give up, take it one step at a time, and—" he began.

"Just do the next right thing?" Anna interrupted.

Mattias nodded. "Yeah. You got it."

Anna smiled. She glanced up when Elsa walked by, talking with Honeymaren.

The campfire crackled and popped as Honeymaren and Elsa sat near its warm glow. "Tell me about the voice," Honeymaren said as she petted a baby reindeer that had wandered over looking for attention. "What makes you so sure they have the answers?"

"Because they speak to a part of me that no one's ever been able to reach," Elsa responded, holding her hand out for the reindeer to sniff.

Honeymaren looked intrigued. "What part is that?" she asked.

"The part of me that's magic," Elsa said.

Honeymaren thought for a moment. "I want to show you something. May I?"

Elsa nodded, and Honeymaren held up a section of Elsa and Anna's mother's scarf and pointed to the snowflakes that decorated it. She showed her the symbols on the points

of the snowflakes. "You know air, fire, water, earth," she said, and then brought Elsa's attention to a diamond in the center that connected them all. "But look—there's a fifth spirit, said to be a bridge between us and the magic of nature."

"A fifth spirit?" asked Elsa, intrigued.

"Some say they heard it call out the day the forest fell."

Elsa's eyes lit up. "Do you think that's who's calling me?"

"Maybe. Alas, only Ahtohallan knows," said Honeymaren.

"Ahtohallan," Elsa said with a small smile. She could remember her mother saying the same thing when she and Anna were children, asking hundreds of questions: "'Only Ahtohallan knows.'"

Their mother had sung a lullaby about Ahtohallan as she tucked them into their beds at night. Supposedly, it was a mysterious river that had all the answers to questions about the past.

As a child, Elsa had wished she could find the river to seek out the answers to her questions. For as long as she could remember, she had wanted to learn more about herself and her magic. Why did she have magical power? Were there others like her out there? And if there were, would she ever meet any of them? In that moment, she realized . . . it was strange, but being in the Enchanted

Forest had made her feel like she was closer to getting some of those answers.

Elsa held the scarf to her chest, hugging it close. She could almost hear her mother singing the soothing tune. She began to sing it, and Honeymaren smiled as she sang along with her. She was surprised that Elsa knew it.

"Why do lullabies always have to have some terrible warning in them?" asked Honeymaren.

"I wonder that all the time," Elsa said with a chuckle.

A distant *BOOM* suddenly cut through their laughter, sending a shiver right through Elsa.

"What is that?" she asked Honeymaren.

BOOM! BOOM! BOOM! The ground beneath them vibrated angrily with each noise.

Honeymaren's face fell. "Earth Giants," she said, quickly rising to her feet.

Chapter 12

*B*OOM! *BOOM! BOOM!*

"What are they doing down here?" Yelana whispered sharply. She glanced over at Elsa.

The ground quaked as the noise got louder and the Earth Giants stomped closer. A soldier dumped a bucket of water onto the campfire, putting it out and bringing a quick cover of darkness to the area.

As the towering Earth Giants made their way nearer, the ground shook more violently. Everyone scrambled as they desperately tried

to hide, ducking behind trees, boulders, and shrubs—anything they could find.

BOOM! BOOM! BOOM!

The Earth Giants continued stomping their enormous feet, walking . . . until suddenly, they stopped.

Elsa carefully peeked out from behind a tree to try to catch a glimpse of them. She could see the staggering silhouette of one of the Earth Giants' faces breaking through the tops of the trees. His cavernous nostrils quivered and twitched as he sniffed the air. She stepped out cautiously, and the face slowly swiveled toward her.

Anna, who was hiding behind a nearby boulder, quickly sprang into action. She grabbed a stick and banged it against the rock, creating a racket. Her plan worked, and the Earth Giants turned away from Elsa, giving up on her scent. They ROARED and began trudging directly toward Anna!

Without a moment to lose, Elsa reached down and let her magic fly, sending it far into the distance, farther than she ever had before. The Earth Giants gradually turned

their heads and stared inquisitively at the snowflakes bursting in the night sky. They watched for a moment and then began lumbering after them.

BOOM! BOOM! BOOM!

Everyone stayed still and quiet, waiting until the Earth Giants had disappeared and they could no longer hear their heavy footsteps.

When the coast was clear, everyone came out of their hiding places, breathing sighs of relief.

Yelana swiftly approached Elsa. "They sensed you. They came here for you."

Elsa nodded. She knew it was true. "I could feel them," she said calmly. "Beneath their rage, wanting help."

"Really? Because I just felt their rage wanting to kill you," said Anna.

Olaf raced over to Elsa's side like a frightened child. He wrapped his twig arms around one of her legs and held on tight. "Oh, don't mind me," he said with a weak chuckle. "I'm just feeling clingy on account of all the danger."

Elsa knew there was no way for her sister to understand, but being in the forest had changed her. She had already faced three of the spirits of nature—air, fire, and earth. And from her earlier visions, she knew there were other spirits. She had risen to the challenges of the ones she had met, and even connected with them. Each time, her power had transformed her and made her

feel different than before. Elsa trusted in her magic and herself more than ever. And if the other spirits came, she would meet them head on.

"I'm going now," she said firmly. "I need to find that voice." Staying would only put the lives of the Northuldra and Arendellian soldiers at risk, and Elsa refused to do anything that might bring them harm.

Anna quickly prepared to leave. She had vowed to stay with Elsa and protect her. There was no way she would let her go alone—no matter what.

Standing beside each other, the sisters felt ready to do the next right thing. Hand in hand, they headed north, feeling the strength of each other's love, support, and confidence, ready to face whatever was ahead. Together.